# ALBERTO RUY SANCHEZ

TRANSLATED FROM THE SPANISH

BY MARK SCHAFER

# CITY LIGHTS BOOKS

SAN FRANCISCO

MOGADOR: THE NAMES OF THE AIR
First published as *Los Nombres del Aire*
by Editorial Joaquín Mortiz, México
© 1987 by Alberto Ruy Sánchez
Translation © 1992 by Mark Schafer

Cover design: Rex Ray
Book design: Nancy J. Peters
Typography: Harvest Graphics


Library of Congress Cataloging-in-Publication Data

Ruy Sánchez, Alberto,   1951-
    [Nombres del aire.   English]
    Mogador / by Alberto Ruy Sanchez  :  translated from the
Spanish by Mark Schafer.
        p.      cm.
    Translation of:  Los nombres del aire.
    ISBN 0-87286-271-2  :  $7.95
PQ7298.28.U96N613    1992
863 — dc20                                           92-29022
                                                         CIP


CITY LIGHTS BOOKS are edited by Lawrence Ferlinghetti and
Nancy J. Peters and published at the City Lights Bookstore,
261 Columbus Avenue, San Francisco, CA 94133
Visit our web site: www.citylights.com

For Margarita

# CONTENTS

*One: In the Hands of the Air*

*Two: The Names*

Unaware, we all enter the amorous dreams of those who cross our path or surround us. And this, despite the ugliness, poverty, age, or misery of the person desiring, and despite the modesty or timidity of the one being coveted, without regard to that person's own desires, which may be focused on someone else. Thus we each open our body to all and surrender it to all.

*Marguerite Yourcenar*

*ONE*

# IN THE HANDS OF THE AIR

# 1

## A FIRM AND SUDDEN GESTURE

*Seen this way, the horizon does not exist; it is placed there by the gaze, a thread snapping with each blink of the eye.*

She would gaze at the line the sky and sea share during the day, the edge they lose when night comes to secretly weave all cloths into one. Now in darkness, she would gaze at a line of stars, a bright, distant line reflected on the water.

*Not even the flight of insects against her eyelids could sever the threads of her gaze: nothing could turn her eyelashes to restless wings.*

This was how Fatma would look into the distance at the farthest blue line where the ocean seems still. And although the sea's deep breathing was not mirrored in her eyes, the air filling her breast seemed to raise waves that fell gently, one after another, on the high beach of her belly. The reddish cloth that covered her almost like a veil imparted the color of very wet sand to the clear skin of her breasts, shoulders, and back. A secret sea was shaping her; so her new gestures led one to believe.

Fatma, fast at her window as if caught between two clouds, inhaling the salt of her desires from the sea, was like a dune submerged beneath the high tide of her dreams. A new world seemed to have emerged in her body, gradually possessing her the way night takes hold of every corner of a house.

Her grandmother was the first to realize something peculiar was happening to Fatma. She had only to glance at Fatma to be sure that a new force — perhaps an evil force — inhabited her. She immediately set about determining what it was that had violated her granddaughter's tranquility and caused her gaze to soar like a bird whose cage is opened for the first time.

It was six, siesta hour in Mogador: the moment when the stars silently realign themselves within the sky's geometry, indicating in their arabesques new paths to men who can decipher such figures. This is the favored hour for reading cards, looking for hidden signs, interpreting birdsongs or the shapes smoke takes as it rises from incense. Like many inhabitants of Mogador, Aisha, Fatma's grandmother, was sure that the writing hidden in all things and in all people is only visible to the human eye at this time of day. To read this writing, she used a pack of cards common throughout the city of Mogador and known as The Deck.

In Aisha's bedroom, on a divan spread with pillows, below a window protected by a large lattice-work screen that concealed them from the outside, Fatma chose, according to the position of the star under which she was born, Venus, the first three cards that would speak of her.

"Just what I feared," her grandmother said when she turned over the first face card in The Deck. "A proud bird now flies inside you, solitary and silent, its beak turned into the wind. You are in great danger. But I don't know yet what threatens you."

Fatma watched with surprise as Aisha turned over the second card, her gesture full of fear.

"The Spiral," she said, somewhat relieved. "The bird within you flies in a spiral: its strength never flags, but grows as it approaches the center it longs for. But danger continues to attend your flight. Accompanying The Spiral is the number nine: the steps that separate you from your destiny, the length of your journey in the spiral, the concentric citadels you must pass."

Aisha lifted the third card as if she already knew which it would be.

"Desire . . . "

Fatma was suddenly seized by the fear that her grandmother would discover her secret. She thought she should get up and run. But her scant hope that The Deck would tell her how to find what she desired held her still. Aisha had Fatma pick nine more cards, which she laid out in the shape of a spiral, at the center of which she placed another four cards, each at the corner of a small, imaginary square.

That diagram corresponds — and this is common knowledge to everyone in Mogador — to the plan of the city: the principal street, The Way or Street of the Snail, which leads by twists and turns from the walls that surround the island to the central plaza, home to the public baths and to the three temples of the three religions that cohabit the port city. To the people of Mogador, the city was an image of the world: a map of the external, as well as the spiritual, life of men. On the circular wall, four towers set over four portals marked the cardinal points: "the universe can be fit in a nutshell by one who knows the scribbled figure that represents it," claims a time-honored proverb in Mogador. A fountain flourishes at each bend in The Way. The fountains suggest that the water flows in a spiral to the baths of the Hammam, cleansing everything and everyone.

Fatma turned the cards over one by one and Aisha read them:

"The first says that a very quiet yet very intense song woke within you the bird that now holds sway over you, but it awoke within a new dream: your longing is woven into a tapestry of dreams that conceals your movements."

Fatma hastily revealed the face of each card, concerned only with finding in them the sure path to what she so desperately desired.

In the seventh card, important because it is always the most informative, Aisha saw the shadow of another bird flying through mist. She also saw the Mount of Venus from which the Moon rose to find its reflection in the water.

Once more, Fatma feared she would be found out and practically turned the next two cards over at the same time.

"Wait!," Aisha cried out in alarm. "Here's what you're looking for. But these three cards speak of the past. You want something you've lost, but it has you in its power. I see another bird, alike yet distinct, that has thrust you into its fiery spiral. That bird is what you seek."

Aisha turned over the last four cards herself, those at the center of the spiral. Fatma felt her heart pounding in her throat, cutting short her voice and breath.

"On your journey, Fatma, you will enter strange dreams: I see a net and a pair of puff fish. I also see an open window through which a wind is blowing. . ."

"Fatma," Aisha said after crying out, "today the song of your bird will again enter the labyrinth of your ear, but you won't know how to distinguish it. You will be very near the bird you pursue, you will almost have it in your hand but will be unable to recognize it because by the time you reach it, you will have lost the colors by which you perceive it. The wind will snatch from your hand what it gave you earlier."

Fatma was even more downcast after hearing the words of her grandmother and felt an inner challenge — enormous, yet worthy of the desire that gripped her. In her window again, facing the sea, Fatma decided to take up the challenge and begin the inner journey Aisha had announced. Her search had begun. She was eager to show that she could indeed recognize the bird that was imperiously setting her own secret birds to flight.

The huge wooden lattice framing Fatma's window sliced the beams of sunlight into geometric shapes resembling stars. A tiny universe, on which Fatma's back was turned, unfolded on the wall behind her.

## 2

# A SECRET IN THE WIND

One could almost see the dryness in the air. That afternoon on the Barbary Coast, autumn announced itself in the wind over the walled city of Mogador. Its unseen surges, long and dry, making their way through the reefs like frenzied snakes, wresting from the scoured stones the sound of something being torn.

And, as happened every year when the season announced itself in this fashion, the birds of the port appeared to answer that sound with caws of alarm. The next morning, the most vulnerable of the birds migrated. That morning the small Moon Tail Gulls, the Sea Turkeys, the Red Crows, the Chilly Storks, and the Dwarf Fowl — those devoured by fish — flew in ever-widening circles around the small boats and vanished. The boats continued knocking their hulls slowly against the dock pilings as the birds disappeared over the horizon, reappeared for an instant, hurriedly approached, then vanished once again.

The city was falling irresistibly before the new climate — cruel bird with cold, transparent feathers — as Fatma at her window heard the wind between the rocks, felt the dryness of the air on her lips, and let her eyes accompany the birds in their indecisive flight.

But Fatma's gaze, obstinate and removed, was a target in flight for thousands of rumors. It was pierced by the arrows of a small city's populace who saw in her fixity the fluttering form of an enigma: a possible secret whose shadow troubled the line of the horizon.

While a hundred rumors crisscrossed the city, the afternoon wind removed the sediments of salt deposited on the wall over the course of the year, lifting large, delicate white leaves off the stone. The moment the leaves of salt were loosened from the wall, the children ran to catch them and then returned home, walking slowly with the fragile sheets in their hands. The sheets of salt never arrived, for the same wind that brought them would snatch them away, and as it sent them flying, reduced them to a dust so fine as to be indistinguishable from the air itself.

Fatma saw the children sink their hands in the stone and gently lift several lengths of fine, spun cloth, which in the sun and from her window seemed splashed with shining stitches. These scraps of cloth exploded in the children's hands without a sound. For an instant, they were enveloped by a luminous cloud that vanished as they waved their arms about, trying to hold on to what they could no longer even see.

With great attention, Fatma watched this scene over and over again, a daily event during that season in Mogador. For she had suddenly begun to observe commonplace events with meticulous attention, finding in them a window onto a world that remained an enigma to everyone else. "Fatma, you look at things as if you'd come from another land," they would say to her, "as if you were only interested in flies buzzing in the distance or birds flying by night." No one could pinpoint the day Fatma's spirit had taken its new and strange course.

When everyone understood this, it already seemed too late and there was no advice to be given nor any clear reason for offering condolences. She was doing everything in a way that exasperated the women and the men, while at the same time inciting them to try to discover what it was that had changed her so.

Everyone in Mogador wanted to know her secret and set out to discover it like someone trying to extract a confession from a mute by interpreting that person's silences: each would put his or her own choice of words in that sealed mouth.

Fatma knew that all around her crude gossip was being spread, but she showed no anxiety, as if all her thoughts were embedded in an unseen cloth, and she knew for sure that no one could grasp her secret because it was made of a light, shining fabric comparable only to those sudden clouds of salt that in the afternoon slipped from the children's clenched hands.

# 3

## SILENT STORM

Fatma had stopped listening to people as easily as if she were deaf, like someone who lets herself be filled by a different music: an enthralling voice, a beckoning song. She didn't cease to see the eyes of those around her, but her gaze would penetrate, nearly wounding, and then withdraw into the distance, opening invisible locks and touching something like the bottom of the air.

She hardly ever spoke: she would utter only the essentials without letting a single superfluous word escape through her troubled smile. At first anyone would have thought she was in a bad mood or feeling sad for a few hours. After a while, one had no choice but to accept that Fatma had gone deep inside herself on a journey of no return and that the change in her was one of those wounds that will never heal.

Someone eventually said that she had been possessed by the soul of a dead person who now demanded her complete attention, and someone else was sure that in her dreams, Fatma had passed through the forbidden doors of the White Palace of the Secret and had remained forever enamored of one of its invisible inhabitants. According to certain women of Mogador, she could only have been transfixed by a spell: distraction or sadness did little to explain what it was that ruled Fatma's eyes.

They went on to say so many things about her, about her window, about the strange way her eyes examined people's bodies: from far away yet deep within, leaving in each person a prickling aggravated by the wind and a deep desire to alter her course, to attract or repel her, to prevent her from cultivating those gestures that refused precise interpretation.

To the inhabitants of Mogador, Fatma soon became more distant even than the body of a foreigner.

Knowing her, they knew her not at all, and unable to discover what her thoughts concealed, those who saw her attributed to her some of their own thoughts: irritable people saw her as irritated, those susceptible to the cold were sure she had pneumonia, people who feared losing things wondered which robbery she might have been accomplice to, businessmen tried to figure out to whom she had sold herself, and those who didn't perceive in her anything specific to blame voiced their thoughts anyway, sensing the alluring moistness of the folds between her legs.

The whispering practically tapped her on the back when she went to the market (the great Soco), to the fountain for drinking water, or to the public oven. She was able to find seclusion in the baths (the Hammam) thanks to its steam and alcoves. And she felt least observed during her brief walk that took her from contemplation at her window down to the edge of the wharf. There, where the rocks are largest, next to the wall, down by the strait where the boats slipped into the port, Fatma gazed at the rippling sea between the rocks.

Those who saw her thought she was searching for something in the water, as she seemed to search for something in the air when sitting at her window. She perceived the same cadenced agitation in the wind which she saw now, quicker, between the rocks: the water flowed in and out of the passageways chiseled through the rocks, swaying the moss that grew in tiny caverns and whose colors drifted from red to green. In the thin foam that vanished before her eyes, Fatma seemed to see a polished window opening onto the bottom of the sea. Under her gaze, the bottom of the sea and the bottom of the air had the same hidden landscapes, the same fleeting inhabitants.

And Fatma seemed to know the precise moment when the transparence of the water and the air merged in the distance, creating that shimmering where suddenly everything is visible.

She would appear dazed after those moments, and there were always people who wanted to ask her about the future, ask advice for closing some risky transaction, or for assurances of future happiness in the face of a dubious marriage. Overwhelmed, Fatma would ignore all those people. They were, in the darkest region of her eyes, like slight and insignificant fireworks in what seemed a long, tempestuous night; perhaps, a silent storm.

# 4

## BURNING AND BEWILDERMENT

Fatma was waiting for and inhabiting the distant move-ments she was able to perceive: she lived in the depths of her prolonged anticipation. And no one seemed to know what absence made her watch the canvas sails billowing along the route the boats took as they left the walled port of Mogador. There were those who came to believe that perhaps Fatma herself didn't know for certain what she was waiting for. Something vague yet indispensable? Perhaps a pair of eyes that watched her as calmly as she herself watched, or some-one as willing to be the object of her gaze as was the distant afternoon. And there were always those who, as soon as they saw her, would want to enter her face to look for the signs that would break her silence: some lines around her eyes or mouth that might reveal for whom she was preparing her smile.

A pensive man who always left the school of the Koran brimming with certainty, became intrigued as he passed by

Fatma's house day after day and saw her sitting at her window looking toward the sea the way she did. He was a young man who was learning with pride and care to see the negation of his own experience as a high virtue, and to find in the Holy Book an explanation, law, and guide to life. Nevertheless, when he encountered Fatma, he was filled with an anxiety the phrases from the Koran in his mind were unable to quell. He began thinking about her even when he didn't see her. She invaded his hours of repose, his hours of reading, and shortly, his hours of prayer as well. But whenever she laid eyes on him, she would look at him with the same indifference — not altogether disdainful — that troubled others. And he burned with bewilderment when he saw her, for he was unable to indentify indifference: a Saracen at heart, he recognized only unsheathed negatives. He longed to find in Fatma's behavior the signs of a possible preference for him, whatever the cost, and he searched eagerly through the Koran for a way to decipher them.

Suddenly the Koran became insufficient to his needs, something his teachers would have considered as grave as finding imperfections in God. So he kept his anxiety to himself, and one morning he awoke before the first prayer, entered the library alone, and opened the sealed case of forbidden books. He had already heard mention of the treatise on love and lovers by Ibn Hazm, and holding it in his hands, he went straight to the chapter on *The signs of love made with the eyes.* "The eyes often play the role of messengers and thus convey what is desired. If the other four senses are doors that lead to the heart and windows that open onto the soul, sight is, of all the senses, the most subtle and offers the most effective results. The gaze repels and attracts, promises and threatens, reprimands and offers encouragement, commands and forbids, strikes at the servants, warns against spies, laughs and cries, asks and answers, concedes and denies. Each of these situations has its own characteristic gaze. . ."

The engrossed scholar of the Koran raced through these lines, ignited by his surprise at discovering that which didn't fit in the Koran, attentive only to his voracious curiosity. He sensed — or rather, desired — that this book held the key to the tangential gazes Fatma directed at him. "A sign made with the corner of one eye only denotes denial of the thing requested."

*But if I haven't requested anything of her.*

"A languid gaze is proof of acceptance."

*That's how she looks, but not when she looks my way. She must use a different sign for me.*

"The persistence of the gaze is an indication of grief and sadness. An oblique gaze is a sign of joy. Half-shut eyes convey a threat. Furtive signaling at the corner of one's eyes denotes a plea. Moving the pupil rapidly from the center of the eye to its inner corner indicates impossibility. Moving both pupils from the center of the eyes is absolute prohibition. . . ." Coming to this line without having found a better answer, he was confronted with Ibn Hazm's conclusion: "All the other signs of the eyes cannot be portrayed, described, or defined *and are understood when seen.*" This was like leaving the aspiring scholar of the Koran seated in midair without a chair. He, who found everything written in The Book, was suddenly being told to look for things no prophet had ever concealed under his robe of infallibility. He understood — or thought he understood — that this was the reason these kinds of books were prohibited.

With his curiosity leading him in other directions, and unable to find expressly favorable signs in Fatma's eyes, he stopped thinking about her. But he began to flirt often with the prohibited books. In time, he would cease being merely a pensive scholar of the Koran. He would privately hold opinions contrary to those of his teachers, would write books that would also be condemned, would found a heretical sect: *Worshippers of the gaze that takes pleasure in resting on the unwritten*. He would write poetry, and would die slowly in a public plaza, having lost all of his followers, held up only by the toothed rope that bit into the necks of heretics who defied the Blessed Word of the Prophet.

If the aspiring scholar of the Koran and future heretic had shown a more careful interest in Fatma's furtive glance, he would have discovered the unrestrained eloquence of the small gestures and other subtle signs that lay behind her silence. He could have created the poetic inventory of the signs of desire, as had Ibn Hazm with the signs of love. For in those moments, the story of Fatma was itself like a tapestry in which were woven the fine threads of various imaginations boiling with desire, her own imagination, of course, being first and foremost among them.

Reading these prohibited books, the future founder of the sect of *Worshippers* would discover a deeply-rooted tradition in Arabic-Andalusian literature, the tradition of the *adab*, the treatise that is at once a narrative and a poem, usually based in large part on the personal experiences of the author. By revealing itself to him, this tradition seemed to be begging him to write the story of Fatma and her desires, to demonstrate for all to see the subtle geometry, the architecture those desires had constructed in the secret corners of several people's imaginations. But the very demons of his calling led him straight down other paths.

Fatma was sitting at her window again, drawing taut the arc of the horizon while the not-yet-denounced scholar of the Koran, intrigued by her eyes, was secretly breaking the lock on the forbidden case. She could never have imagined to what lengths the persistence of her gaze would lead some people, but she doubtless felt a constant rain of questions on her shoulders. And perhaps what she desired was nothing more than a path across the sea that would free her from the many furrowed brows who insisted on knowing what she waited for.

Around her window, long ochre lines muted the brilliance of the whitewashed wall, as if the rain, trapped by the sun against the wall, had left traces of its moaning there, its gilded scratches. Those who passed below Fatma's window and saw her amid the trickling stains that framed her face, saw how those lines illustrated her most languid feelings. Because it was not only in her face but in the things that surrounded her that one had to decipher just how the quiet animal of melancholy was growing and settling inside her.

# 5

## DARK PRESENCE

She saw no one, except her grandmother with whom she lived, and at times even seemed to withdraw from her. The solitude she sought proved disquieting in the port and belied the presumption of some that she was in love. What woman in love would stop seeing her beloved, even if he failed to reciprocate her love? And yet, in the Soco, one of the merchants selling green almonds and unroasted chestnuts declared with great assurance that the signs Fatma exhibited were those of a person who, while asleep, falls in love with someone who visits her only in darkness. The merchant offered proof of his claim by telling what had happened to his grandfather, "who died of a disease of the ideas."

Ahmed Al-labí, his grandfather, a merchant of crystallized figs and dates, made his fortune while a young man. He took the daughter of a caid as his wife, allowing him to expand his business south to the edge of the desert and to the two seas to the east and north. Dissatisfied with the reach of his money, he outfitted caravans that crossed several deserts, traveling from oasis to oasis, then continued by boat and on their return from unimaginable lands, brought silk, gunpowder, gold, and slaves with sad eyes like slender almonds.

One morning, Ahmed Al-labí woke up with an erection so insistent that as the hours passed it became terribly painful. Neither his wife nor his lovers had ever witnessed such resilience and volume, all the more astonishing to see in flesh now at the age of tepid repose. All attempts to appease it proved futile. The most experienced matrons only succeeded in increasing the swelling. The witches irritated it with unguents of old iguana skin. And the doctors were shouted out the door the moment they brandished their honed knives.

Ahmed Al-labí's strange affliction lasted sixty days, during which it didn't relent for a single minute and, on occasions, made him cry out in jubilation and pain just before his veiny pillar ejected the white liquid which every time would seem to dissolve in the air, as if gobbled up by some invisible and insatiable being.

When it was all over, Ahmed had lost forty pounds, slept three hours more every night, and in his dreams spoke sweetly with someone in an incomprehensible language. When awake, he longed to fall asleep again; he was sinking into an increasingly persistent sadness. He lived for only ten more months, though he believed them to be years.

Shortly before he died, the old man confessed to his grandson the dream he had had the night his sorrows began: a slave with almond-shaped eyes appeared as he slept, and her movements were so slow that he followed them one by one with his eyes, as if letting himself be convinced by indisputable arguments. In his dream, a deep desire awoke within him. But the slave left, sinking into a yellow liquid into which Ahmed followed her, eyes closed. When he opened them to look for her the liquid was taking on a reddish tint and then grew increasingly transparent until it acquired anew the consistency of the air. She was no longer anywhere to be seen, as if she had dissolved into the air Ahmed was breathing. He woke up in anguish, his flesh calling out for her. She was everywhere and nowhere, her scent was that of the air, her force that of the wind, her moistness that of the climate, her presence, slight and at times oppressive; always, in its own way, demanding.

After telling his grandson the dream, Ahmed showed him a smooth, colored mark like a tattoo that had lain ever since on the length of his sex like a scar. The mark was shaped like a red, gold, and black spider that grew with each erection without shrinking afterward, as if nourished. Its colors, when exposed to the sunlight, gave the impression of a flame. The spider matured and grew stronger with every month, while his penis grew more and more wrinkled, at last becoming tiny.

Several weeks after that dream, Ahmed Al-labí's emissaries returned from the Orient with their customary cargo. The old man rushed to see the enslaved women, looking for one that might sate his ardor. His surprise turned to rage when he found that, for the first time, his men had returned without a single slave. His rage turned to fear when they told him who had prevented them from doing so, and how.

Arriving at a valley they had never entered before, they sought — as was their custom — the protection of the lord of that place in order to carry out their business. The region was ruled by a thirty-year old woman, owner of lands and people, who had a court, an army, and a library. She interrogated the men from the caravan for a full day about the life of the man who had sent them. For hours she made them describe Ahmed down to the smallest moles on his face, his ambitions, his method of bookkeeping, and many other details. Among them, his passions of the heart and his appetite for foreign female slaves.

When night fell, she concluded her interrogation, saying: "Does your powerful lord realize he could die of fragility, having so extended the abuse of his desires?" She didn't wait for a reply, and retired without looking at them.

The next day she appeared before them with a very beautiful slave with almond-shaped eyes, worthy of disturbing the dreams of the most powerful or the most saintly. Accompanying her were three sisters, terribly alike in their beauty. Each had the name of one of the four winds that blew through that region. They were a gift for Al-labí that his envoys couldn't refuse even as they sensed the danger in taking them, like taking fire in one's hand. One only had to look at them to see that when among them, the desire to lose oneself in the eye of a whirlwind would be uncontrollable. Before letting the women go, the Lady ordered that each be tattooed on the stomach with one quarter of the red, gold, and black spider. Then she handed them over like a priestess officiating at a sacrifice.

Over the next sixty days of the trip, the four slaves died curiously, one by one, as if seized by a millenary weariness. Each one, on her last night, had pronounced Ahmed's name several times in her sleep as her tattoo disappeared. When they checked the dates of their illnesses, they all coincided with Ahmed's dates, and the lost tattoos had come to life on his body at the very same hour. After his emissaries recounted what had occurred, Ahmed Al-labí did not live long. Paralyzed by fear, silenced by sadness, absent in his nostalgia for that dream, frightened by the mark that on windy afternoons almost walked over his stomach, he died staring at a new spiderweb on the ceiling.

When his grandson, the almond merchant, finished telling the story of his grandfather by ritually pronouncing the words: "May Allah have forgiven him," the women listening to him in the market repeated the phrase and, fearing that those mysterious evil spirits, having been named, might appear, hurled into the air the broken gutteral cries that in Mogador extend a welcome to the arriving traveler, and beg benevolence for the criers and their families. The women were becoming increasingly sure that strange and dangerous visitors were lodged in Fatma's body.

As soon as the almond merchant's version of Fatma's afflictions began to circulate in Mogador, they all carefully observed her every gesture, finding in them the movements of another life. At the fountain that flows by the wall — where women with empty buckets can be seen conversing, filling them without looking at the water, and continuing to talk as they walk off with a pitcher under their arm — , one woman remembered excitedly the strange way Fatma's parents had disappeared when she was very young. The other women, terrified, interrupted her before she could tell the story that all intuited, even if they happened never to have heard it before.

That was when one of the women decided to free Fatma from her bewitchment without consulting anyone. And when the night was no longer young, loaded down with herbs and amulets and checking that the moon was in a propitious position, she stole in silence to the foot of the wall by Fatma's window.

Under one arm she carried two wings of a young falcon, the wingtips bathed in the menstrual blood of a black virgin. She swept the air meticulously with the wings, forcing out the malignant spirits. Hanging from her neck was a flat stone whose two colors traced the silhouette of a fortress. This protected her from all enemies. In a leather pouch with sacred inscriptions she kept a mixture of three fumigant herbs. These she used to raise a thick curtain of smoke around the ritual words so that once uttered, they wouldn't be carried off by the wind, and mixed with the smoke; they would take on a more visible consistency.

As she was conjuring the first spells, the salty breeze eddied in a corner of the wall and traveled a short distance with such velocity that as it passed by her, it dampened the herbs and snatched away one of the wings. She grew frightened and clenched her fortress stone in her hand. Disillusioned, she confirmed the next day that her attempt had failed, revealing once more, she said, the great, powerful, and dark presence that inhabited Fatma.

# 6

## THE HAND

It could have been that Fatma's secret motives were more carnal than many believed and that the strange spiritual presence which some attributed to her had actually been a quiet absence. Because the beauty in Fatma's face, in her whole body, was colored precisely by absence. Her hands held things with the fear of losing them, with strength and at the same time with great care, as if she were also afraid of breaking them. Her lips seemed drawn to shape the sound of the most fragile words and to be moistened biting into the flesh of strange fruits, unknown yet foretold by her mouth. The most intimate appetites seemed to rule the tension in the muscles of her long legs, and to have subtly hidden their urgency under the delicacy of her skin.

She walked as if she always knew where she was going, but she always took her time getting there. Sometimes the absences tracing her figure were so great that she could no longer be seen, and people would pass under her window without perceiving her and would feel the fragility of her presence when they spoke of her. In Mogador it was believed she had one foot in another world and that someone in the distance was, with dark powers, calling to her yet not showing her the way. When people mentioned her, they wouldn't say "there she is," but rather, "it seems as if she's there." For the rest, "the melancholy Fatma" was something akin to her own reflection: the image of an image in pain, something barely perceptible in the air.

To some, her open window seemed even emptier when she was looking out of it. For Fatma, however, the window was not the box of her *nothings,* as those who saw her assumed it to be, but rather the door that led to all things and to none. It was the container from which she drew her thirst for everything, since all the volatile absences that formed the air of her melancholy were rooted in the parts of her flesh most easily pierced by the imagination. Roots that took their heat from the belly and their moisture from the skin.

So often sitting at her window she let her lingering fingers slide over her lips until she herself no longer knew whether her finger moved from one side or the other, for she seemed instead to be plumbing profound depths, provoking the eruption of nocturnal senses, the accelerated moisture of her breath. The sea air she breathed in at the window was the hand that gently touched her inside. Sitting up straight, she would fill her lungs, abandoning herself to the air to feel its progressive pressures within her. At the same time, she let her fingers fall on her throat, painted elongated caresses on her neck that became slightly rounded as they descended to meet the rise of her breasts, which offered to reward her with sweet tarrying on the hardness of their summits.

Her fingers follow the rise and fall of all the spirals of her body, coinciding at every moment with the other fingers traveling her body from inside. They recognize each other through the skin like the points of two burning pins that travel the two surfaces of a piece of cloth and char where they meet. The fingers of the air she breathed at her window gave her hands the power to set her body afire. It is the same air that draws her legs taut, that creates whirlwinds between her legs, the days' other climate that rises like the tide, that floats indecisively at six in the evening.

What could those who saw Fatma sitting placidly at her window know, if she herself was uninterested in showing the density of what startled her and the pungent flavor of its barbs. For even when she left her house to walk the streets near the dock, seeking to provoke chance with her uncertain steps, to favor an encounter, she would never allow others to imagine they knew those whom Fatma hoped to meet on every corner; what faces and names they had, who it was who inhabited the air pushed by the sea toward her window.

And it could have been that their backs were slightly rippled and muscular, like that of the dyer whom Fatma surprised bathing in the fountain the morning she left her house earlier than usual to get water, or that they had the smooth waist and vibrant breast of the woman she saw running naked over the rocks before entering the sea, or the gray eyes of the twins who played dice in the spice shop, or the arms, rising light as the night, of the slim black woman who sells milk. The arms that disturbed her every time they reached out to hand Fatma a purchase or her change. But only Fatma could know whether the air that was reaching out its hand to her body and cutting her breath short had a name, a single name that could be secretly uttered in joy.

# MOON IN THE WATER

The white wall that encircles the island of Mogador shines in the night. Sailors approach her joyfully thinking that she is like the moon, that she lies in the water and calls to them. When they are far for long from their white city floating in the sea, anxiety siezes them until they are overwhelmed and, guided more by nostalgia than by the stars, they return and lodge their boats, masts erect, under the archways and portals of the vibrant wall. If the journey home is a long one, they are assaulted in their dreams by the strange image of a naked city, like a lover waiting in a port. Moon-colored, skin moist with longing.

Before they see her, they clearly sense her presence. Yet sensing her like this does not calm them, but rather, hurries them on like quick, blind birds. Until suddenly they hear her: Mogador is a city of ringing voices and her walls are like lips that amplify and modulate her song. Crowning each of the six hundred and sixty-six towers on the wall, a hollow, stone dragon turns in the wind like a weather vane, takes in the sounds of the city through a funnel between its hind legs and hurls them out its throat, transformed into a complex arabesque song, which they say causes those who hear it for the first time to weep with emotion. The chorus of dragons is at times a bellow and at times the city's joy as well as its lament, its keenest song. For the sailors who hear it in the distance, it serves notice that the flesh fortunately is weak and that their restlessness, which a short while earlier was vague and inconsistent, will now take on a delightful shape; like pure, lost, wandering souls who in an oversight of fate are joyfully reincarnated in a moment of true lust. In Mogador, the fleeting desires of a sailor, of a woman at her window, of a foreigner, of a fishmonger, always seem to take shape when sung by the chorus of dragons, and are like a gust of wind that turns to stone as it hits a pool of water, and becomes a fish as it sinks, and as it leaps from the surface flies like a bird that vanishes again in the wind.

Walking along the highest part of the city, Fatma stopped every time a breeze rustled the red veil that covered her back. When the wind died down, a profound silence lasting just an instant would seem to be trying to tell her something. Then up would float the murmur of the street, lost voices, beaten things, barking and bells, laments, laughter, and footsteps: many footsteps that mingled with the distant roar of the waves. Once more the wind would return, turning everything sibilant, and the small silence would again thrust itself into the empty spaces of the mind, entering through the whitest parts of the eyes. Once there, it would convince anyone that everything is alive.

Unconsciously, Fatma would caress whatever was within reach: a smooth stone, an embroidered ribbon, a filigree earring, an olive leaf. Her fingertips would bend gently toward any fabric, as if she could divine something there with her hands.

In each thing, she felt the energy of past lives that hadn't found other bodies in which to be reincarnated, and between her fingers something wounded, like the sex of things, would speak.

Fatma looked up at one of the dragons that seemed to be resting on the wall from its circular trip over the city, and thought that the wind, laden with voices, had slipped between her legs too, and was filling her with a sweet howling that very soon would burst from her mouth. But among the voices that had made their way into the labyrinth of her body, only one moistened it, one alone had known how to open the secret doors of her sex and her imagination.

It was a woman's voice, Kadiya's voice, hidden among all the sounds of the city, that now compelled Fatma to hear in fine detail the moaning of all things. And the empty shell of her ear, like the shell of her sex, was opening to let in the throbbing, the restless murmur of the skin of the air.

Each of her gestures held a slow conversation with everything that crossed her path. Dialogue of surprises. A cat leaps over a garden wall; it carries peacock feathers in its mouth. A pitcher falls into the water; the person who let it drop sighs and complains as she draws it up. Garbanzo beans, broad beans, hazelnuts over burning coals. Two children, eating, approach and hide something: a watermelon. They smash it open under a tree and sink their hands into it, arguing over the seeds. They leave with their fists trickling red water. Even without seeing them, one can hear they are still laughing. A soot-blackened hand has left its full mark on every door: it is to prevent some dead soul from entering. Fatma hears a quarrel between two merchants. A sack of rice is spilled on the ground. Two daggers appear. Shouting intercedes and the men calm down.

When Fatma wished to cross a narrow street, men with banners and tambourines unintentionally kept her from doing so. Behind them, other people riding black and white mules, singing and praying, raised a thick cloud of dust that rose almost to their throats. Fatma had to flatten herself against a wall to avoid being trampled by the procession. She had to press her legs, back, and the nape of her neck flat against the damp, whitewashed wall. It felt cold and the cloud of dust choked her, the clamor dazed her.

Now everything was over in the street and Fatma continued on her way, feeling uneasy until a swift wind blew off the sea toward her. As she calmly breathed it in, she felt it on her face and, smiling, thought she recognized it. There was Kadiya again, and no one but Fatma seemed to feel her presence. The radiance traveling through the air is Kadiya's smile, brilliant in Fatma's memory like certain afternoons when the light seems never to leave, out of sheer contentment. Fatma saw herself shattered into a thousand slivers drawn toward Kadiya's slender, smiling mouth, and the sharp corners of her own mouth held all the magnetized remains of Kadiya's kisses, turned into invisible filings as well.

Woven into those images were several words spoken slowly in the portals of her ears, and they had become one of those echoes that are never extinguished. Kadiya's name itself was already a guarded secret, resonant like all sensations that morning when the two met for the first time in the humid, steamy halls of the public bath: the Hammam.

Like all the women of Mogador, Fatma frequented the Hammam, which opened its moisture in the morning to female bodies only, reserving the water of its afternoon to lubricate the roughness of male complicity. What was the Hammam in the morning? Secret whirlwind: shout, cake of soap dissolved in water, tangled hair, evaporated fragrant herbs, an orange section in a fountain of pomegranate seeds, mint and hashish on full lips, hasty depilations, sandals of swollen wood, red earth for dyeing hair, a bitten peach, obese flowers, vivid tiles, submerged nakedness moving like the reflection of the moon in the water.

Like the public oven, where every woman brings her kneaded dough and talks with the other women as she waits for her bread to bake, the Hammam is one of the places where the women of Mogador can weave together the fine threads of their complicities. None of the three principal religions on the island has succeeded in extending its prohibitions to the Hammam. No phrase from the Koran, the Talmud, or the Bible may be uttered inside its walls, much less written, and — it is assumed — not even thought. The women are careful always to enter with their right foot and leave with their left, as if having taken only one step between entering and leaving. In this way, they place the Hammam outside of space and time. Consequently, the Hammam has its own laws — those of the complete purification of the body, from which one attempts to remove all sadness, as it is harmful, and to train the body in pleasure, which revitalizes. They are the laws of the oldest form of witchcraft which seeks to stimulate beauty and life by concealing the decay of age.

What is illicit outside is, inside the Hammam, as unsubstantial as a fruit whose peel dissolves in the air and one can no longer distinguish where the fruit begins and ends. The progressive temperatures, the bodies emerging from steam as if from their own element, the voices and their echoes, the infallible massages, the immense fatigue and the drowsy arousal, are some of the thousand happy antechambers through which one who frequents the Hammam will pass on his or her aimless journey. Relaxation and cleanliness are not the first things one seeks in the Hammam, although they may be some of its many consequences.

Fatma knew, as did the other women, that in the afternoon when the sex of its inhabitants changed, the very building of the Hammam was as different from the one she knew as night is to day. The murmur one would hear from the street after midday served notice of the transformations that had taken place. If in the morning the laughter was high-pitched and at times shrill — polished like the points of needles woven into the thicket of voices, shouts wavering between sobbing and song — in the afternoon the waves of laughter would grow rougher, culminating in isolated shouts that loudly exaggerated their manly inflections as if wishing to impress the erection of their presence on the others.

But while the arrogance of the afternoon and the hysteria of the morning are the two rigid extremes that keep the walls of the Hammam taut, its many rooms and fountains let loose, morning and afternoon, the labyrinths that favor the existence of intermediate souls and sexes. Over the entrance to the Hammam, entwined in a fine calligraphy that burned in three colors, an inscription in heavy red letters read:

*Enter. This is the house of the body as it came into the world. The house of fire that was water, of water that was fire. Enter. Fall like rain, blaze like straw. May your virtue be the joyful offering in the fountain of the senses. Enter.*

That morning, Fatma entered the Hammam resenting the contrast between the overwhelming brilliance outside and the semi-darkness splashed with color from the small stained-glass windows on the ceiling that distributed their dose of sun over the first room. It was a very large room, one of the largest there, with plain whitewashed walls and a row of hooks at eye level where the women left all their garments. There was a high chair by the door from which an obese and vociferous woman watched over everyone's belongings and collected the money each woman paid to begin her passage through the waters.

Suddenly, Fatma saw more than a hundred different pieces of cloth hanging on the walls. There were more fabrics gathered together in these robes, tunics, and veils than in any storehouse in Mogador. Colors and patterns were displayed there that could never to be found side by side — not even in the chests of merchants from the Orient. Each fabric seemed softer than the next and the difference between each was subtle yet distinct, like the blade of a knife. Fatma imagined her fingers would go mad if they had to find their way among those textures without being able to select or reject any of them.

With the same astonishment, she watched the skin of the women taking off these yards of cloth. She would look to see if there was any correspondence between the softness of certain backs and their linens or silks. She imagined that with time and use, cloth and skin placed in contact, performing the same movements, would transmit virtues and defects from one to the other. That woman wearing a torn shawl around her waist revealed a long and conspicuous marking on her stomach. Where did the wound begin? In the cloth? Which came first, the mending or the scar?

Another woman further off had skin whose color could only have been conceived by a dye-maker who, mixing herbs for several days, could obtain that steely tone glimpsed only in the bricks of a lit oven. When Fatma exposed her belly, laughing at herself, she thought of crushed velvet and slid her open fingers down through the soft, matted hairs to give body to her own black cloth.

As she took off her clothes and felt the sunlight on her body, intensified and colored by the stained-glass skylights, Fatma felt herself touched with delicacy by something that touched alike everyone who entered with her. That light bound her to the other women, dressing her in the same robe and banishing those bothersome angels of modesty who, in contrast to that light, can make even a woman buttressed by cloth feel in need of more veils. Dressed in the colors of the glass, Fatma entered discretely into the other women's conversation simply by looking at them under the same reflections, and following them at a distance, she entered the second room.

There the windows no longer veiled the women's glances and their skin was returned to its original color. The walls were covered with mosaics painted with geometric friezes and voluptuous strokes that mirrored everywhere the bodies' deepest folds, becoming their infinite echo. No longer hiding bodies but breaking down their existence and multiplying their secrets: blurring bodies with images of themselves, granting them an extension more subtle than their own shadows. Fatma let her gaze sink into the holes drawn on the wall — holes that were now her own. She wet the waves of her hair in the water of a fountain and the surface of her drenched skin began to gather reflections that had previously shone only in the mosaics.

In that room the water was not so hot. In the next three rooms the temperature gradually increased until one reached the central room where a large fountain in the middle gushed boiling water. Fatma passed easily through each of those temperatures, knowing they form the ladder leading to the door that finally opens on a region of half-dreams like those she saw for hours at a time from her window each day.

As she entered the central room, she could not help but be

struck by the enormous fountain that seemed to flow down from the ceiling in a boiling waterfall, spreading waves of steam throughout the room. Around the fountain was a circle of stone lions, and one had to climb onto them to fill the water buckets. A liquid resembling mercury poured from their throats and coursed through sinuous channels throughout the room, reflecting the naked bodies in its lazy flow. From the lions' anuses came a thick steam, perfumed and tinted.

There were always women playing among the lions, posing obscenely for the others with the stone muzzles and tails, and those who sat serenely on the backs of the lions, soaping their legs. Once the boiling water was on their skin, the steam that rose from them looked, at a distance and against the light, like white flames.

Fatma entered with her eyes half-closed so as to be surprised by the procession of blazing women on lions, muzzles sunk between their legs. They were demons of the obscene and delicate humidity who placed their hands on the stone in a way so smooth and lingering that they revealed how, just a short while earlier, they had placed their hands on the thighs — never so solid — of their lovers.

Around them, several women talked as they soaked themselves; others soaped one another and many made waterfalls of their voices. As she entered, Fatma saw the steamy shadows moving to the rhythm of the fountain, displaying themselves with the same exuberance as the glazed tiles, sliding from one to another as confidently as ocean currents seem to move through the sea, currents she would now join.

In that fluid circle of women who seemed to walk on the

steam covering the floor, Fatma forgot her everyday body to enjoy the new properties offered her by a seasoned naked-ness. She had moved out of herself as if she had slipped and, as she rose, stood beside her own body. And that slight differ-ence, which obviously only she could perceive, was a wide band over which new joys raced. And if now even her own hands were different and could revive her excitement to the point where she would begin to close her eyes, a short while later that very morning, Kadiya's hands would do the same with even greater skill.

Whereas from the entrance of the Hammam to the room with the great fountain there was a single path on which one was clothed in subtle differences, when one left that profusely overflowing room, concurrent doorways multiplied and one could enter gardens and sunlit springs. They say there are a total of twenty-five rooms in that Hammam, that some are reserved for the powerful and others are segregated spaces: for people with skin diseases, for eunuchs who are still bleeding, for the shamefaced obese, for the uncontrollably violent, for foreigners, for those who refuse to sell their caresses, and for those who can't stand the water and go to the Hammam just to meet other people.

Four gardens were crossed lengthwise by reflecting pools and fountains whose cascades sung in up to twenty-five differ-ent tones. One of the rooms had a reflecting pool which was particularly admired because instead of lying on the floor, it lay on a wall on which architect-apprentice-magicians had succeeded in causing an enormous curtain of water to fall from the ceiling to the floor so slowly — practically motionless — that one could see one's own reflection more clearly than on the surface of a standing pool of water. In another room, scenes had been painted on the walls to excite the lusty imagination of anyone who looked at them; or anyone who touched them, since the walls had been made in relief so that the people who adore representations of the burning in the flesh might linger against them.

In another room, the paintings were not merely the blaze: they served as initiation to the fire. They illustrated to passersby the thousand ways to caress the penis with the lips, to envelop the clitoris with the tongue, to suck and lift and bite and caress, in succession or all at once, to fall from bed and get up without having to separate, to shake out obsessive stiffness and to drive away premature softness, to drink again from dry wells and to dry those that trickle down to the knees.

There were rooms dedicated to massage in which the most common was not particularly exciting. It consisted of a robust masseur who linked his arms and legs back to back with those of his victim, the person being massaged lying face down. The masseur drew his body taut as a bow until the joints of the other person cracked. One by one, the masseur collected thirty-two cracks from each patient. After each crack, the fleshy man made a noise with his mouth that sounded like a sheet of paper being torn or a dry kiss, he let out a phrase (whether it was a prayer or a curse no one knew for sure,) and shifted his position slightly in search of the next report. In the morning, the masseuses were valued and sought not only for their skillful musculature, but also for the absolute roundness of their bodies. They were like great balls of flesh that absorbed delicate bodies as they rolled along and caused bones to yield the intimidation of their accumulated tension. They also strove to make the joints articulate the sound of a crystal bell that falls and rolls around on a carpet.

There were rooms dedicated to the dyeing of hair and the palm of the hand with a reddish or yellowish earth called *rássul,* which is found only on the outskirts of the city of Fez and is dissolved in rose water or orange blossom water. Eyes were also painted with charred bitter almonds to darken the eyelashes and with kohl to line the eyelids. Fatma preferred to use kohl from the Hammam rather than the merchants in the port, since the kohl from the Hammam was prepared by the women at home, following all the precautions the merchants didn't observe. One had to gather together coral, clove oil, the pits of black olives, a pepper corn from the Sudan, and small kohl pebbles. Most important of all, everything must be ground by seven pre-pubescent girls or by a woman "who has passed the time when liquids boil in her body," as the *Book of Recipes and Advice of the Women of Mogador* instructs. The ground mixture should be sifted through a coarse cloth and the fine powder that is obtained is dissolved in cat's urine to give a greater shine to the eyes, and is applied with a very thin piece of straw in two lines on the eyelids.

In that same room Berber women displayed their tattoos in their entirety, and brides, their depilations, taking care that the spices, fragrant herbs, and goat's milk poured into the water didn't alter the painful markings on their skin. Beauty achieved through suffering, however slight, — but always flaunted — is in Mogador beauty most complete. The display of mutilated flesh, of intense pain glimpsed through makeup, thrives among the women of Mogador with infinite complications. Fatma knew that exuberance well, and since she didn't display the deep tattoos of the other women, it seemed to have little to do with her. But the air of melancholy that gradually came to possess her after that morning would itself become a spontaneous form of displaying pain, of adorning herself with her sadness like an insect that spreads its wings in the afternoon, imitating banana leaves or plum blossoms.

It was still too early that morning for Fatma to display great joy or sadness, and she let a black Egyptian woman named Sofía line her eyes with kohl. This woman knew all the secrets for arresting fertility, sterility, impotency, and other calamities. While she attended to Fatma's eyes, Sofía gave advice to a forty-year old woman with drooping skin and a flabby waist and spirit. "To hold on to your husband, you will do everything I tell you. Very early in the morning, while he is still sleeping, and shortly before he wakes, repeat in his ear three times: *May heaven burn this forgetfulness from your head, may the floor shake, hurl you, and wake you up deep inside me.* You must do this for eight days without him hearing you while awake, and the first thing you give him to eat in the morning must be a piece of date that has passed the night inside you. But he can't suspect a thing. After a week you will see his passion growing. To keep him from spending it on others, you must steal the sheet that a black woman and man have dampened with their sweat as they made love. Burn it at the foot of your bed. Mix the ashes with rain water that has not been walked upon and apply a little each day to every one of your orifices. If you can't get the sheet dampened by two blacks, you can use the sheet from a prostitute. But in either case, the sheet must be stolen for its ashes to work. The people who dampened it at night can't suspect a thing, before or after. Should anyone else know when and how you do all this, the power of the spell will dissipate."

Fatma was impressed by the docile appearance of the woman who involuntarily nodded her head as she listened, clenching one fist without letting go and touching her throat with the other hand. Fatma imagined her undertaking the long and arduous task which Sofía had charged her with, but saw her stopping in anguish before one of the obstacles. The vision of a defeat was on her face, as if the woman herself was sure her future was inhabited by impossibility.

Fatma also imagined her overcoming all the obstacles and being disappointed, having seen no results, asking herself through the passing years at what step, in what movement, in what word of the charm she might have erred.

Fatma was frightened by her desperation, despite having seen the woman in the marketplace besieged by suitors she despised. At that hour of the morning, Fatma could still enjoy the luxury of believing it absurd to persistently desire the love of a person one can't have nearby, while quickly rejecting love that is close at hand.

When Sofía realized that Fatma was growing very tense watching the desperate woman, she hastened to make up her eyes without knowing for whom she was adorning them, and sent Fatma off with a kiss on the forehead.

Fatma was afraid to enter several of the rooms in the Hammam that, at the same time, fascinated her somehow, and as she walked by them, she stood on the threshold watching indecisively. In the snake room, thirty completely toothless and lavishly oiled cobras slithered among hundreds of leather pillows and the naked bodies of those who, morning and afternoon, partook of their privileges. There were those who had their favorites and others who had theirs reserved: snakes that were only taken out of their baskets in the presence of their owners. Fatma dreamed once that she was laughing, entwined in snakes, with the same nervous, high-pitched laugh she had heard other women emit at that unceasing sensation between one's legs. Fatma never dared touch the snakes, although something very powerful attracted her to them. She was horrified by those insistent eyes and those aggressive knots which the snakes allowed to be untied only when hashish smoke was blown on their ears.

But even though Fatma didn't enter that room, caresses bolder than those of ten snakes would leave their infinite mark between her legs and a slipknot, which she didn't yet suspect, was about to tighten around her chest, cutting her breath short, causing her to cast longing glances from her window. Like the sailors longing to see Mogador transformed again into a naked reflection under the water. If the chorus of dragons on the wall could sense sounds long before taking them into their resonant bodies, they would be howling now — like a pack of wolves howling at the moon — to warn Fatma. Kadiya was near.

# 8

## FALSE TWILIGHT

Once a month at noon, a very tenuous purple mist filled the air of Mogador. From the rooftops, it looked strangely as though the white walls were emitting a ruddy radiance. They called it "false twilight" and it never lasted more than fifteen minutes. It vanished as slowly as it came, pulsing to the beat of the sea against the sand. It anointed everything as it entered the city, touching all things almost without touching them, breathing the same still air as they did. For that reason, when a lover proceeded slowly but surely, that person was praised as being "a false twilight," "a purple cloud," or "a great wave of blood diluted by the wind."

As the reddish cloud entered the houses, it surprised the women when they opened the door, when they felt a presence at their backs and spun around, when they held out the palms of their hands and the mist flowed over them, when their lips felt more swollen and the mirror showed them to be a deeper shade of red, visibly colored by the cloud, almost bitten by it.

That morning, Fatma had already passed through the steam room and the pool of many temperatures. She was entering one of the most peaceful gardens in the Hammam when she felt the aggressive moisture of the "false twilight" on her lips. She recognized the sensation on her face that she had always enjoyed as a child. But now, dressed only in the steam of the thermal springs, she felt that warm, nebulous pressure on her other lips as well.

She tried to defend herself against that unfamiliar touch by feigning indifference. But as she advanced into that cloud where time stood still, she grew more and more vulnerable to the deep caress her young skin seemed to have been calling for now for some time. The caress that some kind of midday demon — or angel — was lavishing on her with the boldness and enthusiasm of someone who finally arrives at a long-awaited appointment.

Fatma pretended not to hear the music that was beginning to play in her body. For some time now her strings had desired hands that might temper them, but she tried to insure that her ears remained faithful only to external demands. In the distance, from every minaret, people shouted the midday prayers toward Mecca whenever the purple cloud made its appearance, following the prayers with phrases from the Koran describing Mohammed, sword in hand and on horse-back, vanquishing all the demons in the form of a cloud. Another religion in Mogador rang the metal flower of its bell towers in a special style called Angelus, which was supposed to have the power to dispel the demons that appear out of nowhere when, like an invisible sphere, the day splits in half. According to the ancient books of this sect, when the bells peal an angel of light beheads a legion of demons whose blood evaporates and, dissolved in the air, colors the city as it floats overhead like a cloud. Immediately afterward, the same angel cleans it up, casting the midday sun, reflected on the blade of its sword, over all things.

Another sect begins breaking rocks when the reddish mist arrives, certain that in one of those rocks is a picture that depicts the cloud vanishing. They are peculiar rocks that contain landscapes or immodest scenes, a few battles, and many starry nights. People belonging to that religion are sure that the ideas of human beings can be grasped through certain rocks and that man's most intense thoughts — his desires — take shape inside the sacred stones. Some interpreters of the igneous scriptures claim that man's past and future can be read in the heart of the stones. Others worship a kind of stone that grows when well-nourished by the man's loving ideas, and they say that the entire history of humanity is nothing but a conceit gradually imagined by one of these living rocks, the most ancient of them all. Certain rooms in the Hammam have walls of stone covered by erotic scenes that were not painted by human hands. They say the walls were originally blank, but over the years have absorbed the obscene forms that pass through the minds of those frequenting the Hammam. However there are also those who think that in fact the walls themselves desire. That their surface is a kind of fresco of a mind on which are drawn the longings of a supernatural being

— perhaps a mineral god — living in the Hammam, overexcited by the bodies that offer themselves to its waters.

All the religions of Mogador perceive the "false twilight" as threatening and deploy prayers and rituals to protect their followers. While they are in the Hammam, the women of Mogador remain temporarily outside the sphere of obligations of any of the religions, but also outside their ritual protection. That is why they sing together when the "false twilight" catches them in the public bath. Then each one sings to the cycles of the moon, to the fate spun at night by women, to the highest tides of the month, to the blood that secretly filters down every thirty days, to the whims of the body sailing to the strict time of the seasons, to reason's nocturnal submission to the obscene empire of jealousy, to the confused joy of an unexpected amorous meeting outside of time, to desire's voracious and ever ambiguous imagination.

Fatma listened to that song without thinking that it spoke of her as well. Her new destiny as a woman was just beginning to display its profile even as the recently abandoned universe of her girlhood was retreating into the distance.

Still feigning indifference to the appeals of her skin, Fatma slipped away unnoticed to the doorway of one of the many terraces overlooking the garden. There, two women isolated from the world by the depth of their abandon gazed at one another without touching.

One of them, seated on the padded rug, sweetly sang the story of a Saracen love tempered by the violence of a conquest and the blood that avenged an abduction. Her voice alternated with the sounds her fingers drew from a fragile and very beautiful object covered with strings. The other woman, stretched out on thick cushions, naked as well, listened to the song with the attention of someone in love, commenting softly with two or three words now and then without interrupting the song, almost singing along.

It wasn't long before Fatma realized that the two women were in love with the same man who at times scorned them and at other times took them without any signs of passion and with undisguised disdain, speaking without fail of other lovers better satisfied. But Fatma also realized that this same unrequited love, much larger than the target of their keen desires, joined them in a higher dimension, strange, voluptuous, and complicit. That they made love to one another in the depths of a night without memory, as if a single invisible snake, one whose skin was alive with the stars of the dying day, bound them together, forming a living bridge between the labyrinths of their sex and feeding them with images of a common destiny traced in the skies. Fatma could not avoid hearing the discreet music emanating from the movements of the two women governed by a single desire. She watched them kiss and suddenly felt enormously scared. She shut her eyes and imagined herself abandoned in the room of the oiled snakes, two or three of them climbing her legs in slow spirals. She opened her eyes and saw nothing but the reddish mist while feeling once again, and stronger than ever before, the dusky moisture biting her lips. She no longer knew what was inside her and what was outside.

# 9

## NINE STEPS

A spiderweb would take nine days and nights to fall from heaven to earth. And it would take the same time to fall from earth to the underworld.

Hesiod

It is well known that he who succeeds in descending the nine fundamental steps without falling has mastered the silence of his nine senses. He has broken down the doors that kept the world from the nine orifices of his body. He has opened himself to the world.

Ibn Arabi

### One

With her eyes wide open, terribly tense in her desire not to blink, Fatma walks through the clouds of steam in the Hammam. A purple mist climbs her thighs. When she sees it, she feels the colored steam once again threatens to bite the lips between her legs. She is afraid to lower her eyelids because she knows that at the first moment of darkness something very hot, like that reddish sun she has believed on other occasions was inside her — though never with this intensity — , will make her envision herself covered with snakes like the women she saw a short while earlier in one of the forbidden rooms of the Hammam. She imagined herself walking in a secret ceremony toward her own sacrifice, entangled in long bodies that move and mingle with her own. Her two hands are toothless heads that watch with their knuckles and bite with their fingertips. Her vagina is the nest from which surge all the drenched dreams of snakes that draw spirals on the slope of her buttocks as they gently submerge her body in their slithering. Over her moist back, a thousand scales reflect their rainbow and her skin is whipped all over by hundreds of double tongues, tiny and unrestrainable. Like small growing stones beyond the point of bursting, her nipples ache.

## Two

After blinking once, she opened her eyes convulsively. She brought her hands to her breast, covering it with a slight caress; actually, protecting it from the scene that even now with her eyes open was still vivid in her mind: the thousand tiny tongues that made her tremble and dodge small, secret convulsions as she walked, perceiving with every step the beating of her blood as it rushed through her veins. Every movement Fatma made was like the first impulse of an invisible hand rising to touch a body that has forever held it in its dreams. With every step, she crossed a jungle or desert with a mirage on her brow.

## Three

Covered by that ritual gown that no one could see, Fatma passed in and out of the dense clouds that compressed the room in the Hamman from within, slicing through them with the steely gleam of her nakedness. Her appearance between two currents of steam was that of a silent bolt of lightning. Just as Fatma perceived the bodies of the other naked women who crossed her path with this same surprising force, anyone who at that moment had looked into her pupils would have seen something like two startled gods watching an intense lightning storm from the sky. Everything she looked at seemed to touch her inside, illuminating her, lighting her veins on fire and evaporating her blood.

## Four

And so she walked on without knowing clearly where she was heading, with a rippled fury at the base of her belly, led by her attraction to the radiance, sounds, smells, and above all, that strange light emanating from the deepest folds of some women. Her gaze searched for that light and took refuge in it for an instant until everything was again hidden by the steam, as if her eyes were closing under the heavy eyelids of a cloud. She had entered a kind of white night and was now one of its ghosts: little more than a shining breeze looking to take form, imagining a body in which to take shape. Suddenly the time came when the purple mist, the "false twilight" that seized Mogador once a month at noon, abandoned the city. Fatma would have wished to follow it, or rather, leave with it, letting herself be carried by its deliberate, possessive momentum. The mist was linked to an awakening of her senses.

## Five

Given back to the whiteness of certain walls and the steamy canvasses entangled and held in the air, Fatma felt as if she were in the heart of a rock, travelling through its veins as if through live passageways momentarily and deceptively quiet, held in the middle of a breath. Fatma was in the middle of a night of clear stone, a night inhabited by dreams of the stone itself: its secret drawings, its destinies traced as if on the palm of a hand. Though she didn't know it, Fatma was now prisoner of an inexorable geometry: she was a predestined point, a line in the universal arabesque; she was a picture drawn in foam in the sea of desire, a silent tide obeying the moon.

## Six

The water in the fountains fell with intentional force and rhythm: they had been tuned to draw music from the water.

The tones resonated in the vaults, corners, and skylights as if other instruments were playing them back: not echoes but rather, new voices. The light also entered the rooms mastered, measured, and sung anew: it was treated and interpreted like the water. Water and light were interwoven with the slow voices of the women, with the songs some of them were singing, with the lingering lines of their bodies and the sweat on their skin. Between two tangled curtains of steam, like an unexpected sound, Fatma caught sight of a dark back she had never known and whose smooth forms increasingly absorbed her gaze. Fatma saw Kadiya's back and shoulders before discovering — or being discovered by — her full lips: before feeling, with hesitation, her mouth's undeferable call. She tried to lower her eyes and could not. She tried to close them but it was too late: Kadiya was already engraved inside her.

## *Seven*

Two gazes crossed like the arcs of a vault designed long ago. But their gestures interwove differently: Fatma settled into a passivity that asked to be pleased, just as an image at the bottom of a drinking vessel asks to be discovered and admired when the vessel has been drained. Kadiya came to her like an elaborate but swift waterfall: a filigreed cascade.

## *Eight*

When they regained their sense of time, Fatma's pale fingers and Kadiya's very dark ones had caused a dense forest of black and white branches to grow between them, interwoven like illegible calligraphy. They had met each other in silence and loved each other in the same absence of words: the light and moisture of their bodies spoke. They said what many words are ultimately incapable of saying. On another terrace, a woman sang a very old song by Ibn Zaydun in a very keen, sorrowful voice: "When your eyes see what can no longer be seen, and your hands touch what can no longer be touched, your eyes will no longer be your own and your body will no longer be your own, poor woman, possessing and possessed."

## *Nine*

Fatma wanted to hold the taste of that silence in her memory, and she closed her eyes as if by doing so she could definitively consume Kadiya's presence and turn her into a melody that keeps springing to one's lips. And soon she would discover that she did well in wanting to conserve those moments, for although memory is fragile and slippery, it is perhaps less so than skin and feelings: when Fatma opened her eyes, she found that Kadiya was no longer by her side. Again and again she searched the Hammam, but to no avail. Again and again she returned to the corner where Kadiya's scent had impregnated the cushions, until the scent itself was diluted in her memory.

*TWO*

# THE NAMES

Where desire is all-inhabiting
air is to the window
as fish to the net

> *Formula engraved*
> *over a window in Mogador*
> *in the 12th century.*


If dreams weren't an awakening,
a certain kind of awakening,
they would always have passed
unnoticed.

> *María Zambrano*

# 1

## THE WINDOW: *FATMA*

Fatma returned home that morning, never suspecting that she would never be touched by Kadiya's gaze again. Fatma would never see her in the Hammam, though she walked for hours around the room where they met and assiduously smelled the perfume impregnated in the fabric on which they had violated the visible surface of time. When she asked about Kadiya, everyone insisted they didn't know her, some with indifference, others as if hiding a shame Fatma was unable to decipher. When she walked through the streets looking for Kadiya, it only emphasized her absence. She couldn't understand why Kadiya eluded her.

She felt as abandoned as she had earlier felt fulfilled, as unjustly rejected as she had been willing in her surrender to Kadiya, as mysteriously alone as she had been surprised by her double joy.

These sensations intertwined within her like threads in a

very thick fabric. At the same time, she felt that everything she saw from her window was also made of this deep cloth.

The few hours she had spent with Kadiya were retreating in time but were not vanishing. Yet, the joy of those moments had grown so subtle as to be perilously fragile. Her light and recently acquired melancholy was formed of those sudden shocks that are not exactly the blackest of sorrows: a neutral layer that dampened her enthusiasm for daily life; on the other hand, a layer that sheltered the vivid images of her keenest excitement, hiding it from sight, holding it captive for her alone. This layer that covered her became a dark current in her dreams, a river of drenched fabric moving beneath and before her, gently carrying her along.

But it was not in her dreams that she let herself be steered by the force of her spirit in an extended glide, but rather in that intermediate region where she was neither completely awake nor yet asleep, where colors, forms, and sounds came to her with a more subtle touch, new and enveloping. She was in the region of semi-sleep where everything that is close, rather than simply being at rest, leads toward distant depths where nothing exists in isolation, where everything moves and is moved.

There she would skirt the impossible with ease, would dream while awake. This state of half-opened eyes was what most revived her longing and allowed her to place it light-heartedly in everything around her. Because in her semi-sleep, even the plant in her room was inhabited by Kadiya's movements.

Its leaves were shaped like slender drops, like her fingernails, like the base of her belly. The green of her eyes was too obvious a comparison but Fatma made it as well; so was the position of certain branches that lifted toward the window like open arms. She didn't know with what to compare the white and red flowers, so she simply contemplated them uneasily.

But what most shook her was the obvious characteristic of this plant sold in the city market under the name Impatience: its fragile stems and the surface of its pointed leaves turned toward the light with a swiftness and elasticity uncommon among plants. Fatma saw in this exaggerated inclination toward the window a cruel coincidence with her own life: that was how she looked at everything, although Kadiya surely wasn't looking everywhere for her like that.

Somehow it hurt her to find in that plant such an exaggerated dedication to the light-filled air that entered through the window, and every once in a while she would turn the pot of earth in a rage, pointing the leaves into the shade. If during the day, the entire plant twisted its stems back toward the window in less than an hour, straining visibly, it hurt Fatma even more. In her passion to impregnate everything with Kadiya's absence, she filled everything with her presence, filled a vacuum talking to herself about Kadiya. And she made everything take part in that secret dialogue. The only resistance came from a plant, her Impatience, belying Fatma's reassuring dream with its impetuous motion. Thus, while the objects that surrounded her could speak to her of Kadiya, her Impatience only allowed Fatma the repetition of that phrase which poured from her lips during her painful awakenings:

"Stop dreaming your dream of me in my dreams."

Sometimes she sat at the window holding a book, but the printed letters were too fixed and didn't let her sail easily through their absences. At other times she found a text that at least in parts compelled her to go on seeing the other shape of the world in her half-dreams. But there were not many books she could hold in her hands, and her enthusiasm for a certain poem, song, or character refused to last.

One night, moved by a passage that stayed with her even after closing the book, she began to write an endless letter to Kadiya. The sentences fell one after another like waves. She wanted to tell her everything and at that moment was sure that it would all fit on the tiny nib of her pen.

Even things she had never thought of before were being written down in her agitation. But suddenly, her illusion that Kadiya would read those lines began to recede as quickly as it had come. She stopped writing the letters but didn't stop thinking them. She would have liked to throw them into the air and let chance place them before Kadiya's eyes, plaster them on the walls of the streets so that everyone would know of her urgency and would repeat it to Kadiya. She would have liked to find herself pursued from some window and written by a restless hand.

There was a mirror in her room and when she saw her reflection there, it seemed too slight, as if the mirror were defective and didn't show the image of the most important part of her, which was the image of another woman. She began walking through the streets again, defying the law of chance encounters. As the day wore on and she grew increasingly aware of the weave that surrounded her, she found it more and more unbearable to go on looking. But during the moments that surrounded her dreams when she was no longer waiting and her eyes lost their tension, a hand would reach out from the empty chair she kept in front of her and snatch away her tranquility.

In a whirlwind no one can see, all the cloaks of the air were torn apart one after another before her eyes and from them came Kadiya's hand, inviting her to take it in her own. Of all the movements to which Fatma's half-dream of Kadiya's voluptuousness had recourse, that gesture — the hand of desire being held out to her — was the only one that returned, lone and insistent, that slipped through the shadows of the skin's urgency and surged into Fatma through the slits of her half-closed eyes.

In the moment Fatma remembers, the two of them were lying on the cushions in the Hammam when Kadiya interrupted their caresses and sat up, looking at Fatma with one of those fixed gazes that almost enters the body. She extended her left arm to Fatma like an imperious summons, an absolute "come to me," then took her by the shoulders, embracing her again, but this time deepening her caresses with a possessive fury that never engulfed the minutest expressions of her tenderness.

The same hand searched for her in the street or as she sat on the dock in the sun or waited in the market for others to pay for their fruit. The hand held the thread that moved her legs and braided the paths she walked. It was a hand that watched, that reached out from behind to touch her when she sat down, from in front when she walked, and from inside when she was at her window. Sometimes she let the deceptions of the hand lead her to other bodies. An adolescent her age penetrated her hurriedly beneath the trees, caressing her clumsily and without listening to her. A woman who looked like Kadiya kissed her without subtlety, demanding the movements of a man from her fingers and hips.

In this way, she frequently let her desires confuse the faces of their true inhabitants and more than once had to flee in the middle of a kiss or after already having undressed without understanding her sudden disgust.

So she shut herself up in her house, facing the walls of the city that held back the insistence of the waves. At night, the incessant pounding found its way to her ears, and when she was in bed, that sound opened the door to her dreams.

Fatma entered the night like someone starting a secret task at a prearranged signal. One could say she slept almost out of obligation. She behaved as if, while asleep, she were doing a monotonous day's work that bored her. One might think that at night she was accomplishing all the activities her melancholy kept her from doing during the day. She would go to bed full of energy and get up tired, with sweat on her brow and the gesture of someone dispossessed. It seemed that in some corner of her dreams, Fatma elaborated mysterious obects that were snatched away from her as she woke. And that was waking up for her: the surprise of finding herself empty-handed.

Arriving on the first shores of morning, she was awaited by her grandmother, who always woke up earlier than Fatma to offer her the words and smiles that eased her descent into the obligations of the day. The two of them lived in the house that had belonged to Fatma's parents until the day they had decided to sail to the continent to resolve some business pending there. They never arrived at their port of destination, although they had left in haste as if late for an appointment. The ship was never heard from again. Many people had it still sailing in intermediate regions of a sea about which geography still knows nothing, guided by stars which even the astrologers conceal or forget.

Those who saw Fatma at her window and knew the story of her family imagined that it was her parents she kept looking for in the air, and that one day she too would embark on a voyage to sail with them outside of time. Faced with that possibility, many people in Mogador refused to board the same boat as Fatma. Some were even afraid to get close to her when she was walking very near the sea. There were anxious widows who, when they saw Fatma staring at the horizon, turned and strained their eyes to see the distant points at which she gazed and claimed to have seen her parents calling to her. They also swore they had seen a sail swollen with the breath of specters.

But Fatma didn't even know her parents. She was six months old when they left and if she knows about them and remembers them, it is only through the stories told to her by her grandmother who, as she woke Fatma, always told her of the conversations she had had with them in her dreams. Aisha, her grandmother, filled her own absences by fully abandoning herself to her nocturnal sediments, which allowed her to make it through the day mourning a little less or bearing a lighter shade of black that didn't oppress her spirit. When she woke up, her grandmother could concede herself smiles that Fatma only allowed herself at night, while asleep.

Aisha engaged in leisurely conversations with the dead. Every night someone would visit her, shining with the flawless face of youth conferred by nostalgia. At night, she peopled the emptiness of her days with happy ghosts, trapped in moments of joy so well established that when morning arrived their new and momentary absence would leave no scars. Sometimes distraction and an evasive memory led her to converse with distant people who had not died. At times like those, instead of clearing up her confusion, Fatma would take joy in seeing how her grandmother peopled her graveyard of smiles as she pleased. Deep down, she also wanted to believe in those visits and think that Kadiya might come one night to whisper in her ear.

There were moments when Fatma felt her melancholy to be uninhabited since Kadiya's face no longer came as easily with each wave. She watched the clouds insinuate a smile that was at times Kadiya's. She would stare at nothing, at the small, empty space hidden now by the clouds as they broke up. She never ceased watching the holes in the sea that floated through the air to her window. She was watching.

Around her window, Fatma would impatiently weave the tablecloths of desire on which her life was being served, eaten, and scattered.

## 2

# THE FISH: *AMJRUS*

From her window, Fatma could see the section of the dock where boats are hauled out of the water to have their hulls repaired. Every day the fish auction was held amid the damaged boats in a circle of wood shavings. Ship owners and merchants came to negotiate over large quantities of what would later be sold in the small market by the dozen. In the shadow of a newly-painted hull an obese man shouted out the fishermen's bids: the type of fish, weight, and final price.

The clamor of the fat man and his buyers lasted a few seconds at a time. It looked like a quarrel among stutterers in which many would speak at once. Amjrus was known as the shouter, and was so fat that when he sat on a bench, the bench seemed to disappear, so enveloping were his rolls of fat. After each sale the fat man sweated and wiped his forehead with a red handkerchief he tied around his immense neck. Between the fingers of his left hand were scraps of paper the fishermen gave him, attractively describing the qualities of their fish. He stuck each one between two fingers and his swollen fist seemed to sprout vanes with which he fanned himself. When he stopped shouting, he threw the damp pieces of paper to the ground, the ink washing out of some of them.

Before the auction, he had the fishermen place samples of their wares in an attractive box, making sure they didn't include the biggest and most deceptive fish. He capriciously kept the fishermen in line, not allowing them to include any fish with colors that displeased him. He detested green with a hint of yellow.

Fatma enjoyed watching from afar the procession of fish being auctioned: the shapes and colors were those of a new gliding of her feelings. But the anchored gazes of the men at the auction would pull her from this drifting — above all, that of Amjrus, who seemed to transform his obesity into an erection whenever he set eyes on her. From then on, Fatma would let the radiant colors of the fish in their crates infuse her only through the corner of her eye and reluctantly averted her gaze so as not to find herself in the hands of the men who mocked her or tried to touch her as she passed by.

Amjrus had been observing her for quite some time, and saw how she filled herself with melancholy's larvae. But apart from her intermittent sadness, he had noticed the tautness need had lodged in her body. He mistakenly believed that the voices of the flesh are also for those who overhear them.

He saw her body quiver with every step she took and would begin to imagine her undulating over his rolls of fat. He was aware of the repugnance his swollen bulk produced in women, and each time he tightened his belt, he seemed to set afloat an old grudge against all the women who had wrested existence from his desires. Fatma's indifference reddened him from within, it irritated him as he walked and set the roughest part of his skin aflame. He wished to believe that when Fatma looked at the fish, she was actually looking at him, and in an effort to force the coincidence of their gazes, he too looked deep into the crate of colors enameled by the water trickling off the scales.

As he walked among the fishing boats, overseeing the selection of samples, Amjrus watched Fatma at her window and tried to adjust his movements to what he believed would be most pleasing to her gaze. He made broad gestures as he walked, leapt up the stairs with feigned agility, and spoke to everyone with a display of authority.

When in the holds of the boats, he ceased acting as if he were in the spotlight but continued to be ruled by similarly contrived preoccupations. He came to believe that when he went down into a hold he would suddenly find Fatma naked, lying on top of the fish. His imagination was as coarse as his arms.

Even the fishermen who accompanied him on the inspection could guess the form of his bloated obsessions, for Amjrus fell like an avalanche on a pair of puff fish which, placed one beside the other, made him think — so he said — of a girl's buttocks scarcely larger than his two hands. Agitated, he put them in a sack without another word and continued on his inspection.

Frictions would always arise at the auction and Amjrus was

supposedly in charge of smoothing the transactions, but he threw his weight against those who didn't give him additional money for having secured them a deal. Lately, he was constantly coming into conflict with the fisherman who one day had tried to assault Fatma and who wouldn't forgive Amjrus for laughing at him when the girl threatened him with her sandal. When the auction was over, he and Amjrus went to fill up on beer to float their grudges to the surface.

Amjrus tried to explain to him that he had laughed in order to gain the sympathy of the woman passing by and not to accentuate the fisherman's humiliation. The latter was not particularly convinced and felt obliged to take revenge on the fat man. And on her. He only withdrew his threats once he had insulted and slapped a fellow who was passing by the bar, light-hearted and cheerful, a friend of everyone and of no one. Amjrus and his resentful companion ended up singing arm in arm, and talking about women the way they would talk about fish in the market. Fatma sprung to their lips piled high with adjectives and desirous exclamations, insults and threats.

Finishing a glass of beer, the fat Amjrus suddenly got up to go to the bathroom where he pulled from a bag the two puff fish he had found in the boat's hold. He pressed the fish together with his two hands extended and pushed between them the greasy object of his short and violent masturbations. In pain from the chafing of the scales, impatient with the extensions of his body, he grit his teeth in frustration as if to transmit the rigidity of his jaws to the indifferent flaccidity hanging between his legs. He left the fish lying on the bathroom floor, as if by throwing them away he would rid himself of the irritation caused him by the excited but indifferent volume of his body. He returned to his companion at the table full of empty glasses and knocked several of them over as he tried to put a few coins on the table so he could leave at last. And so he stumbled out, determined to follow the street that led to Fatma's house.

Arriving under her window, he realized she wasn't there. He was determined to attack her, to shout in her face all the obscenities he could muster, to take off his clothes and shock her with his hanging rolls of fat. He was starting to get discouraged looking up when he realized Fatma was coming down the street alone, heading home.

He immediately thought of raping her. He waited for her to get closer. Now she was practically at his side. Now she was opening the door to her house and walking in. With the sound of the front door ringing in his ears, the obese man choked down his saliva and bit his tongue for having delayed while he had weighed his doubts.

In a fierce struggle with his drunken feet, he walked toward the hidden part of the dock, the other side of the landing stage where he would come every Saturday as he did that day to the ship hung with red lanterns and its market of women. Amjrus frequented the ship with loathing, compelled each time to reconfirm his lack of appetite. He was known but not well loved there. He wouldn't stand for the jokes about how his belly hung down, how he spent little on liquor and left just the amount agreed upon for the night and not a penny more. He was generous only with his reprimands and contempt, the way he was now treating the woman who had put up with him on this occasion, and who watched him wake up in a bad mood and laboriously get out of bed to leave the ship in anonymity before night departed.

Amjrus looked at the woman, who was already awake and observing him silently. It seemed to him as though she lay at the bottom of a stairwell, that perhaps she didn't even deserve her pay. That if it weren't for the fact that the boat's owner was a friend of his and she one of the owner's favorites, he would leave without paying her. In short, he had slept the whole time. As he pulled the money out of his pocket, he thought again for a moment of Fatma and compared her to this woman who had accepted his company. He resented the woman in the window and felt contempt for the woman on the ship. But one he placed on a pedestal and the other he ground underfoot in the mud.

With each bill he counted out, the aggressive contempt he felt for the woman watching him increased. He felt relieved and superior to her because he aspired to lay his body over another woman, one who had never been to this side of the dock. The obese man believed that by desiring Fatma, he could impregnate himself with the qualities he saw in her. Such was the crudeness of his thinking.

He would never have imagined that Fatma desired the woman lying right before his eyes, who, more than any other, could stop Fatma in her tracks. Amjrus finished counting out the money and almost out of habit asked her: What's your name? The dark-skinned woman was called Kadiya. He put the money in her hand and left the ship, lamenting the fact that at that time of day the Hammam was not yet open to men. He would have to wait until afternoon. He belched as he descended the gangway, scratching his belly.

# 3

## THE NET: *MOHAMMED*

A few hours after Amjrus left the red circles that radiated from the bobbing lanterns, Mohammed also abandoned the ship. Day had already broken and the round, red tablecloths thrown down by the lights shrank until they hid inside the small boxes of illuminated glass. The lanterns jingled as Mohammed walked down the gangway.

The Mohammed walking this way isn't the Mohammed who sells fabric, nor the one who makes clay pots, nor the one who tends goats, nor the one in the wine store, nor the husband of his aunt, nor any of the many other Mohammeds to be found in Mogador. He is one of the fishermen Mohammeds, and not the one who tried to molest Fatma in the street and then got mad at Amjrus. He never would have dared cast a bridge to her in the street. When he wished to meet her after seeing her at the window, he told his mother, who, thanks to her neighbor who knew the neighbor of Fatma's grandmother, arranged for him to see her in the drawing room used for obligatory family visits behind a table of coconut pastries over which Mohammed now didn't hesitate to cast his broad bridges.

As Mohammed walked down the gangway, provoking sounds from the lanterns, he thought about how it was becoming time to establish his own household and to look for a wife. It was very uncomfortable arriving at his mother's house from the brothel and getting dirty looks and scoldings from the woman who always knew where he had been. Furthermore, he thought, it would surely be more pleasant on his arrival from the red ship or from fishing at dawn to enter a place soothed by the dream of a wife who waited for him without conditions or rage. Seeing the gentleness of Fatma's manner, he thought ever more seriously about her as the hub of his domestic plans.

He wanted to go to the Hammam but almost four hours remained before it would open to men. While he waited to enter the baths, he went to his mother's kitchen to be served breakfast after being lectured. He hoped to spend a few hours afterwards mending his fishing gear. His mother asked him if he had seen Fatma again. He didn't want to admit that the woman in the window fled from him; he preferred to think that Fatma's evasions were nourished by modesty rather than disgust. He told his mother about Fatma's eternal silence, implying that her silent agitation, her embarrassment when he stood in front of her, was a timid symptom of her great interest in him.

His mother agreed with him, wanting to be certain that her son's proposals could be of inestimable worth to a young lady who so resembled her and who would surely make a home just like she had made before she was widowed. What terrified her in her son's preference for the woman in the window was the curse that had hung over her since the disappearance of her parents.

She was afraid that one day Fatma would embark on a journey with her son to that region from which there is no return. That place where Fatma's parents were supposed to be, waiting and calling for her. Mohammed calmed her by saying that the business about them calling was certainly false, that Fatma's melancholy was due to her being secretly in love with him. Nevertheless, he promised he would never board a boat in her company, just as a precaution.

He left his mother's house convinced it would be wise to speed up his preparations for the wedding. He was sure that if he hit on the right approach, Fatma would quickly agree to share the seasons with him. He began to make small repairs on his boat, certain that he would soon be desired by Fatma. He interpreted her gestures according to the two or three sentences they had exchanged one afternoon. He told her what he wanted, after his own fashion: "How I would like to see your shoes placed under my bed every night." She felt this to be more offensive than the time the other fisherman had tried to touch her in the street. Rather than pawing her, this man wished to anchor her beside him, to wrap her up forever. But she didn't respond with violence. Blushing, she told him that she would always keep her shoes in her own closet, and ran off. Mohammed wished to read into that answer a very timid and modulated *yes*.

Sitting on the dock, he serenely began mending his torn nets while letting images of Fatma in the window come to mind to the rhythm of his needle. Mohammed believed with increasing insistence that her melancholy gaze sought him and no one else. His fisherman's imagination made him set sail toward his own future, dragging everyone else along in his nets with strange confidence. Sometimes, as he watched the late afternoon sky, he would convince himself that the sun was waiting for his attention in order to set.

Now as he sewed the torn nets, he let himself be carried away by the calculations of his desire. He saw Fatma as his wife, waiting for him at his mother's side among the women dressed in black who fill the dock when it's time for the fishermen to return. He saw children holding Fatma's hand. He saw himself descending from a bigger boat than the one he had now.

As he painted and repainted the old orange walls of the boat which had previously belonged to his father, the colors and shapes of his new embarkation blended in his eyes with each coat of paint. He calculated how much his profits would increase with a bigger boat and was certain that he would rise accordingly in the estimation of the other fishermen and his neighbors. They would even treat him better in the brothel, and his woman, with Fatma's face, would be viewed in Mogador with respect; she would be the wife of Mohammed, the owner of the big orange boat.

Not far away, among the rocks near the dock, Fatma was letting her imagination float on the sea. She gazed with her usual serenity, seated in the spot she frequented as often as her window. Her feet were in the water when she saw a sliver of wood coming toward her, shedding fresh paint like drops of oil on a pool of water. When she connected the orange color floating toward her with Mohammed, who was painting his boat that very color at another section of the dock, she yanked her legs out of the water as if a keen loathing had made her cringe. She felt as if the bitter taste of the paint were in her mouth, as if Mohammed's thoughts were stealthily creeping up on her. She ran home, unavoidably crossing the dock where Amjrus and then Mohammed saw her pass by. Fatma saw the fat man and puffed out her most obese indifference, but when she saw the fisherman, she felt in her disgust like a needle stuck in a fresh pile of dung. With the demands of both men in mind, Mohammed's seemed an intolerable obscenity. Perhaps because that was very likely where her future lay.

When Amjrus saw her pass him with indifference, he thought of returning to the brothel that night, and that in the meanwhile he'd go to the Hammam. But when Mohammed saw her running by, he thought it wouldn't be long before he would make her his wife, and then she would run to him, perhaps to bring him his food. He was sure that by offering her the matrimonial rugs, he would be removing her from a situation in which she felt uncomfortable. He preferred to believe, as had others before him, that by including a woman in his plans, he was saving her from some extreme danger and so she would always owe him her life — every corner of her life. Thus Mohammed could remain convinced that Fatma was indebted to him on a higher plane: one of those debts that are never paid in full.

He hastened to mend his nets and run off to the Hammam. It was now time for it to open and when he saw Amjrus heading toward the center of the city, towel in hand, he tried to catch up with him so they could walk together to the baths. If he eventually bought another boat, it would be to his advantage to be on good terms with the officer of the auction, and knowing how money made Amjrus's eyes shine, Mohammed calculated that it wouldn't be difficult to buy his favors. As he was not able to put away the cans of paint and gather up the nets quickly enough, he decided to meet Amjrus inside the bathhouse, perhaps next to the great fountain of hot water or in the gardens. But it was in a corridor that he first saw the broad figure coming his way and rushed to cross paths with him. Amjrus allowed Mohammed to explain the magnitude of his plans and the more the fisherman talked, the lower the businessman set his price. The more interesting or audacious was Mohammed's portrayal of his calculations, the more they seemed filled with air and saliva to the expert in prices. He almost burst out laughing when he thought that for a moment he had taken the fisherman's plans seriously and sought to make money off them.

Amjrus began to lose interest in the novice fisherman's conversation until suddenly he saw how to charge him for his initiation into the hidden side of transactions in the fish market. It would cost him a hundred times what the experience of disillusionment was worth. The fat man waited silently for the fisherman to exhaust the attractive features of his offer until he felt he had nothing more with which to tempt Amjrus. Thus he magnified Mohammed's willingness, who now wished to acquire the obese man's protection at any price. He was already offering more than he had planned. Seeing that the possible profits from the fisherman were even slimmer than his young, muscular stomach, the fat Amjrus turned his attention from money to Mohammed's firm flesh. It seemed to Amjrus that the fisherman's wide hips were somehow similar to Fatma's hips, and he took him to the padded rugs in the back of the Hammam.

The entire conversation took place in a corridor crossed by the clouds of steam that spread from the various rooms and filtered the light, causing it to fall in waves instead of rays. Amjrus focused on the drops that nibbled at Mohammed's back and couldn't restrain himself when he wished to lay his broad arm against those moist shoulders. He hugged Mohammed, feigning paternalism, but was already letting him know that in addition to money, he would have to pay with the availability of his body. Very soon, Mohammed would lose his boat and all his fishing gear.

They walked together, leaving behind a white wall on which a tile arabesque spoke of the geometric destiny of mankind and of the secret algebraic formulae that under Allah's rule govern the meetings and partings of those of us who live under the moon.

Amjrus and Mohammed continued walking on at an apparently amicable gait. While the fisherman spoke to him very seriously of business, a silent smile crept over Amjrus's face: a smile that extended into the air, that grew sharper until it became, to his mind, the long and distant thread of the horizon.

# 4

## THE AIR: *KADIYA*

The woman who crosses the horizon on the wind-blown ship of red lanterns — Kadiya — has left as her only history the trail of her repeated absences. She traveled from port to port with the same regularity as day follows night. Hardly anyone in Mogador knew her outside of nocturnal transactions, and the few people she could speak to of her past quickly forgot it in the passage-ways that lead from pleasure to dreams. Of Kadiya it is known only what could be repeated by those who have on occasion held her close — but so close that they are the most distant from her.

From many mouths a legend is formed and each person finishes it to suit his own tongue and keeps it or forgets it according to his appetite. It required an insatiable person, an adolescent in love with Kadiya, for her story to leave the ship intact for the first time, defying the vigilance of the red lanterns that color everything, and begin to pass through the city's mouths, which inquire into everything.

In the silence of the night that allows the light to dilute its thickness as it departs, the swift words shaped on Kadiya's lips passed through the air like tiny darts. Each sound shone on the moisture of her mouth, absorbing the gaze of her nocturnal companion, who, as the day broke, was on the highest rungs of hypnosis from which one descends only with great difficulty. Though sleep and fatigue plugged his ears with a dense ball of nothingness, Kadiya's voice strung together the silence of the night, and as she withdrew, she wrapped it in a long, silk thread. It bound his inertia and strung him without distraction on his fascination for her like an invisible shell where her words resonated more clearly than anywhere else. They were practically written on the air, practically fit in the palm of the hand and leapt to the mouth.

She realized that this new person sighing for her had been crystallized in one of those prisms that multiply reflections, granting more dimensions to a yes or no than they could possibly have. He was submerged in the gleaming glass box opened by the woman who at that moment was initiating him in the immersions of sex. He was unaware that his initiation — like any other — gave him a new innocence rather than took it from him. He was the innocent young man in love with the first smile that had gladdened his body. She spoke with the knowledge that the ears listening to her were more disposed than most, but without letting herself be strung along by the illusion that this was anything more than a fleeting joy.

She was gratified by the unaffected tenderness in the eyes of the young man who caressed her slowly, but she wasn't bound up in silk thread nor did her companion's voice weave itself inside her. Kadiya told her story to him without simulation, sensing that soon he would not give the same weight to her words: the new thirst that had been awakened in him would send him to springs where his first drops would mingle. She and he were the same age, sixteen years old, but while Kadiya already knew where the air currents blow, he was only beginning to realize that his body was moving in the air.

Shortly afterward, when the story of Kadiya began to circulate from door to door in Mogador and to be told in the plaza by the all-knowing elders who every day collected money from passersby for telling stories accompanied by pantomime, it was the version of a resentful lover who feigned disinterest when in fact his interest was multiplying. The young man initiated into the pleasures and pain of passion had kept the first promptings of his turbulent fascination a secret, and thought that by revealing the secret, he too would be freed from the fervor of these promptings. And so, feeling that a distance foreign to his desires was being imposed on him, he used his power to violate distance with indiscretion.

Kadiya, in turn, had revealed the colors of her past to him, not so much out of a lack of caution, but because she had begun to care no longer whether her secrets were known outside the ship of red lanterns. It was now four years since she had been sold to the owner of the ship and the harrowing events that had finally put her there were beginning to heal in her memory. When she saw how on the first shore of morning the profile at her side began to distinguish itself from the darkness of the room, she allowed a pleasant confusion to invade her: the mild enthusiasm of feeling once again that fresh joy other dawns had brought her.

For some time she had been moved by the way things would separate from each other as the intense light began to arrive, sowing its slight differences. One dawn in particular contained her memory of the others: the first morning she had watched it rain in the Zagora oasis by her father's side, just over four years ago.

Her father was the one who led the nomadic Tassali tribe as they crossed the desert. He had led them beyond their customary migration this time, pushed on by the enormous drought that had wiped out life in the oases they passed by every year. Zagora was far to the north of their routes, where the desert suddenly came to an end. But at that time a rainfall lasting three hours had surprised everyone in Zagora, for it hadn't rained there for fifteen years.

Five or six groups of nomads rushed toward that zone where the sand had been covered with tall, slender leaves of vegetation offered hesitantly to the wind, moving with the same uncertainty everyone in Zagora felt as they saw their landscape suddenly transformed. The next day they also saw one hundred goats brought by the nomads devouring the plants and flowers the sun had not been able to consume. Vengeance was not far behind.

People living in towns and cities always mistrust nomads: they come and go without worrying about the order of those who live between corners. They don't have churches. They are regarded as heretics or evil-doers, tolerated when they serve the cities by crossing the desert with their caravans, or by doing business in goats, arms, and cloth.

In Zagora, the days of rain made many people happy, above all the Tobib, the oldest of the elders there, who climbs the mountain every day before the sun rises, sits on a rock that over the years has rubbed smooth the seat of his tunic, his djellebah, and begins to look at everything he can see. That is his daily job; he is sure it is important and everyone in Zagora seems to believe so. The first thing he does is to look toward a point in the darkness which he alone knows, and, from there, invoke through prayer the illumination that will allow him to separate day from night and the sky from the earth.

Everyone in town knows that the Tobib is on the mountain when day breaks and that his job is much harder during the winter: old and tired, he can't prevent the days from growing shorter during the cold months. Some people complain about him, saying that when the Tobib was young the days were brighter and things were more colorful, because he was less concerned about making light than he was about giving color to everything.

His day's work begins when everything is so black he can't see his hand in front of his face, and little by little he begins outlining the things he knows. He says that "people's silhouettes are the hardest because one must have a good memory: the townspeople would get angry if their faces weren't the same as the day before." After outlining the palm trees in the valley, separating the houses from the mountains, and giving profiles to the people who pass by early, he begins to concentrate on the colors of all the things he has differentiated. At first everything is very gray but then the Tobib's powers create colors so intense that each thing continues coloring itself out of sheer momentum.

It's typical for things nearby to have brighter colors than those far off: the Tobib's powers weaken over distance. It's no longer known whether those mountains in the distance are blue or black. The most important thing in Zagora is that the Tobib climb the mountain, for his absence would leave the city white and cause people to lose their edges.

"The white panic" was what they called the enormous fear that swept through the town of Zagora for a whole sunny day when the Tobib failed to climb down the mountain after his work was done. When they went searching for him they found his body dyed red and run through with a dagger which no one in Zagora recognized. When the news of his death raced through the population of Zagora, the first thing they thought was that the next day they would enter a new life, everyone, black or white, indistinguishable from the sand and other things. They didn't even know whether this would be existence. Some preferred to die right then and there and threw themselves in a well or slit their wrists. Others had already begun to die when they saw the first bodies and their fear grew.

Following the trail of blood, they discovered that the dagger belonged to the Tassali nomads, Kadiya's tribe. Convinced that the curse brought down on Zagora for the following day would be cleansed if they sacrificed all the men of that tribe, they took them captive and killed them one by one, praying with faith and zeal before the massacre. The women were raped and sold to slave traders and the owners of floating houses of prostitution.

The nomads had been in Zagora more than two weeks before the death of the Tobib. It had been five days since the fruits of the rain had been exhausted and since then the nomads had been trying to leave. But every morning some mishap prevented them from doing so. Lost goats, an accident, bad weather, a bad omen. The guide of the Tassali feared that these obstacles would continue, and passing by the temple of Zagora, he heard the story of the Tobib on the mountain.

By the fifth day their departure had been delayed, he was convinced that the Tobib was set on outlining their tents in the same spot every morning, and in this way his tribe had been taken prisoner by that man's gaze. He hoped to free his people by bathing the eyes of the Tobib in his own blood, the way they handled goats that led the herd astray.

That is how one elder in the plaza of Mogador told what was once Kadiya's past, the violent incidents that would eventually bring her to the ship of red lanterns where she was bought to be sold again every night. Many people listened to the old *halaqui* as he elaborated on details and exaggerated his gestures. He would give each character names common in Mogador and received more money than when he told other stories.

Even Fatma dropped him a large coin as she passed by. She was slightly shocked when she heard the story and didn't, of course, connect it with the woman she had known in the Hammam. It seemed to her like all the stories told in the plaza: as foreign to her as any she had heard there. But as she walked away from the plaza, she felt something like a jostling of her memory: as if she were on the verge of remembering a word that never quite reached her lips. Something in the story drew her attention in a special way.

She no longer heard the tale in the plaza, but the characters and incidents spun out in the old man's gestures continued to inhabit her; they took on a life that her consciousness could no longer control. She thought about how she had never seen it rain in the desert, that maybe it was worth the trouble to see this oddity; that the woman in the story lost her father as she had lost hers, but that at least this woman knew her father. In any case, when she heard the story, she planted her feet a little deeper in her sadness and consoled herself by thinking that fortunately nothing like what had happened to that nomad woman, flung into the absence of her whole family and sold on the floating brothel, had happened to anyone she knew and loved.

Then she thought that she had finally remembered what it was that had seemed to touch her memory so hesitantly when she heard the elder's tale. She thought it was simply the memory of a sensation like that of a recently finished conversation continuing on in silence. It had happened to her often that upon reading the final pages of a book, she remained intrigued about the fate of the characters, even if they had died in the novel. The plot itself or the description of a character, a certain scene or image, awoke in her constant visitations of what had been left behind.

And she thought the same thing was happening now with the story of the nomad woman, who would come to mind again with her other daily obsessions. And so, in her mind as well, the desired figure of Kadiya passed very close by the nomad woman sold in Zagora. By a coincidence so keen that it passed Fatma unnoticed, the two different stories momentarily crossed paths in her body — two stories that were actually one, and which, had she accepted them together in her mind, would have offered her the longed-for key to draw near again to Kadiya's pleasant gestures. But the air snatched the bold idea of this coincidence from her as well. She had heard the flight of the bird she was searching for, but had not known how to distinguish it.

Fatma would walk home as the afternoon grew dark in Mogador. She saw, as people placed their weariness in the new expanse of the shadows, how even the features of the severest faces seemed to acquire a vast calm. She thought that at this late hour the inhabitants of Mogador entered a kind of second existence, similar in every way to the existence the characters of concluded stories would take on in her mind.

She too enters that silence as she enters her house with the night.

CITY LIGHTS PUBLICATIONS

Prévert, Jacques. PAROLES
Purdy, James. THE CANDLES OF YOUR EYES
Purdy, James. GARMENTS THE LIVING WEAR
Purdy, James. IN A SHALLOW GRAVE
Purdy, James. OUT WITH THE STARS
Rachlin, Nahid. THE HEART'S DESIRE
Rachlin, Nahid. MARRIED TO A STRANGER
Rachlin, Nahid. VEILS: SHORT STORIES
Reed, Jeremy. DELIRIUM: An Interpretation of Arthur Rimbaud
Reed, Jeremy. RED-HAIRED ANDROID
Rey Rosa, Rodrigo. THE BEGGAR'S KNIFE
Rey Rosa, Rodrigo. DUST ON HER TONGUE
Rigaud, Milo. SECRETS OF VOODOO
Rodríguez, Artemio and Herrera, Juan Felipe. LOTERIA CARDS AND
        FORTUNE POEMS
Ross, Dorien. RETURNING TO A
Ruy Sánchez, Alberto. MOGADOR
Saadawi, Nawal El. MEMOIRS OF A WOMAN DOCTOR
Sawyer-Lauçanno, Christopher. THE CONTINUAL PILGRIMAGE: American
        Writers in Paris 1944-1960
Sawyer-Lauçanno, Christopher, transl. THE DESTRUCTION OF THE
        JAGUAR
Scholder, Amy, ed. CRITICAL CONDITION: Women on the Edge of
        Violence
Schelling, Andrew, tr. CANE GROVES OF NARMADA RIVER: Erotic Poems
        from Old India
Serge, Victor. RESISTANCE
Shepard, Sam. MOTEL CHRONICLES
Shepard, Sam. FOOL FOR LOVE & THE SAD LAMENT OF PECOS BILL
Solnit, Rebecca. SECRET EXHIBITION: Six California Artists
Sussler, Betsy, ed. BOMB: INTERVIEWS
Tabucchi, Antonio. DREAMS OF DREAMS and THE LAST THREE DAYS
        OF FERNANDO PESSOA
Takahashi, Mutsuo. SLEEPING SINNING FALLING
Turyn, Anne, ed. TOP TOP STORIES
Tutuola, Amos. SIMBI & THE SATYR OF THE DARK JUNGLE
Ullman, Ellen. CLOSE TO THE MACHINE: Technophilia and Its
        Discontents
Valaoritis, Nanos. MY AFTERLIFE GUARANTEED
VandenBroeck, André. BREAKING THROUGH
Vega, Janine Pommy. TRACKING THE SERPENT
Veltri, George. NICE BOY
Waldman, Anne. FAST SPEAKING WOMAN
Wilson, Colin. POETRY AND MYSTICISM
Wilson, Peter Lamborn. PLOUGHING THE CLOUDS
Wilson, Peter Lamborn. SACRED DRIFT
Wynne, John. THE OTHER WORLD
Zamora, Daisy. RIVERBED OF MEMORY